Ellie & Ollie Eel

HAPPY READING!

This book is especially for:

_____

Suzanne Tate,
Author—
brings fun and
facts to us in her
Nature Series.

James Melvin,
Illustrator—
brings joyous life
to Suzanne Tate's
characters.

Suzanne and James in costume

Ellie & Ollie Eel

A Tale of a Fantastic Voyage

Suzanne Tate

Illustrated by James Melvin

Nags Head Art
Number 16 of Suzanne Tate's Nature Series

To Mark

loyal son,
ardent supporter

NATIONAL AWARD WINNER

***Ellie & Ollie Eel* was a First Place winner in the National Federation of Press Women's 1995 Communications Contest.**

Library of Congress Catalog Card Number 94-67925
ISBN 1-878405-10-1
Published by
Nags Head Art, Inc. P.O. Drawer 1809, Nags Head, NC 27959
Copyright © 1994 by Suzanne Tate

Ellie and Ollie were big, slippery eels.
They were long, skinny fish
covered with tiny scales.

Their skin felt as smooth as velvet
because the scales were so small.

Ollie lived most of his life in a bay near the ocean.
But when Ellie was young, she swam and
wiggled her way up a river.

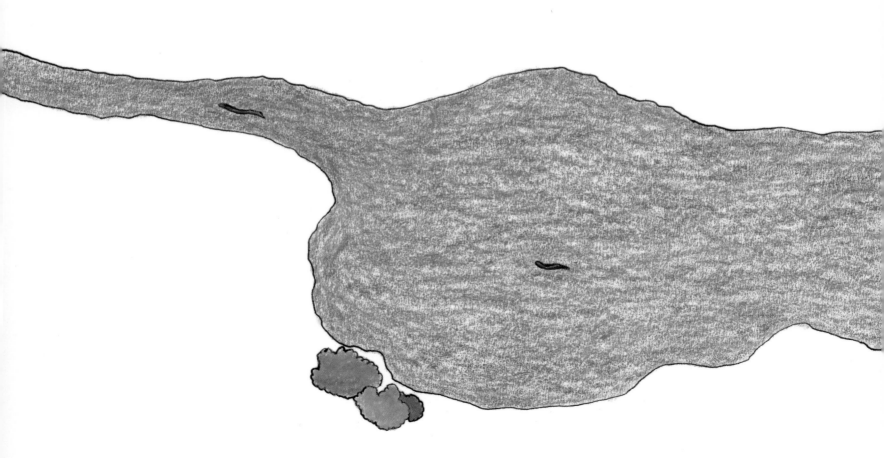

Ellie stayed in the river until she was seven years old.
Then, she swam down the river to the bay.
It was there that she met Ollie.

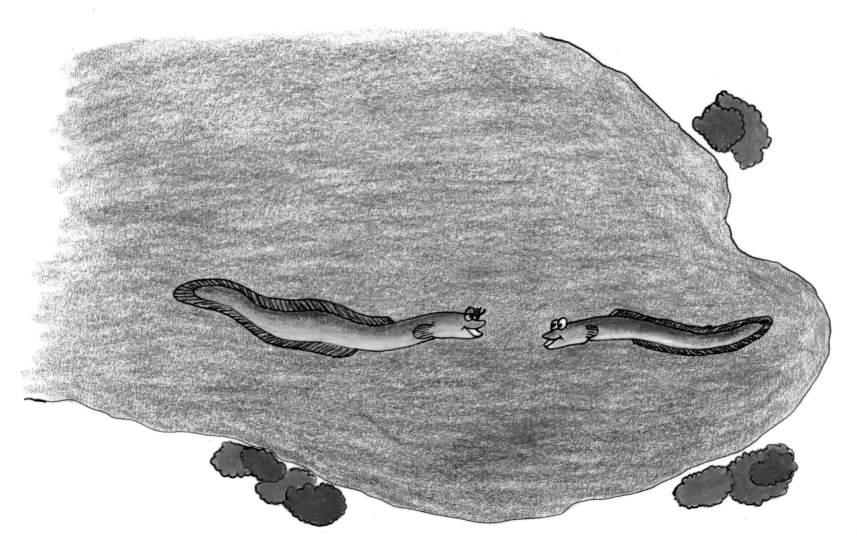

"Hello, how are you today?" Ellie asked.
"I'm hungry," Ollie replied. "But I know
where there are good things to eat
at Tate's Landing."

Tate's Landing was a seafood store
beside the bay.

"Oh, you really shouldn't go there,"
piped up other eels in the bay.
"You might get caught in one
of Mark Tate's eel POTS."

Ollie didn't want to listen to them!
"Come on, Ellie, let's swim over to
Tate's Landing tonight.
We can find some tasty scraps
of fish and crab there."

That night — when eels like to feed —
Ollie swam closer and closer to Tate's Landing.
Ellie thought that it was not a good thing to do.
But she followed behind him and didn't say a word!

With his slippery skin, Ollie swam
and slipped easily along the bottom.
And his sense of smell was the very best.

Ollie could smell things he liked to eat
as he swam near Tate's Landing.

Suddenly, he slipped inside one of
Mark's eel POTS and was trapped!

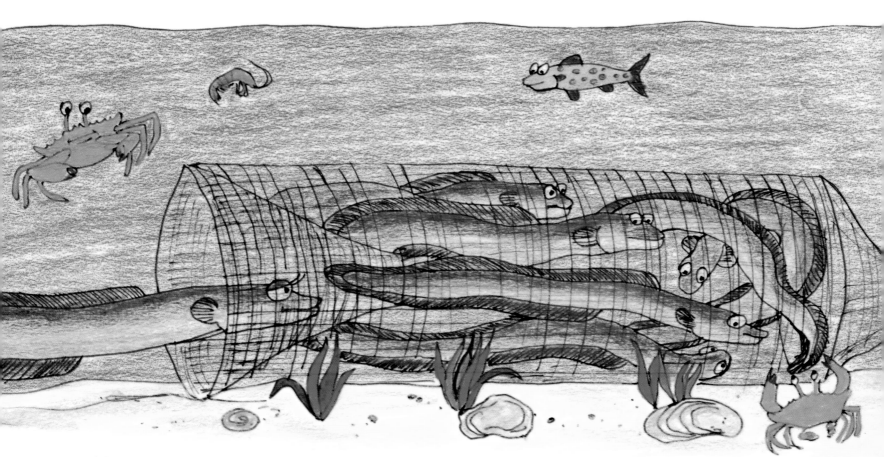

Ellie swam up near him.
Right away, she was trapped, too.

Other eels were in the POT, squirming and squirming. "Oh, you shouldn't have come in here!" they cried. "You won't be able to find your way out."

Soon, Mark came along and lifted the POT.
He sold eels to FISHERMEN for bait.
So he was happy when he saw all those eels!

A FISHERMAN and his wife came to Tate's Landing.
They gave Mark a "big nickel" for a bagful of eels.
(A "big nickel" is what Mark called a coin worth 50 cents.)

They put the bag in their truck.
And down the road they went.
Ellie and Ollie and all the other eels
squirmed and squirmed in that bag.

Suddenly, the bag of eels broke open!
The FISHERMAN'S wife screamed and
jumped up and down in the truck.

And those slippery eels just kept on squirming!

The FISHERMAN stopped the truck and
opened the door.
"Let's get out of here!" cried Ellie.

And Ellie and Ollie and all the other eels
squirmed out of the truck.

The eels wiggled their way into the water
near the road.

They quickly swam until they were back in the bay
— but away from Tate's Landing!

Now, it wasn't long after their escape,
that a strange change came over Ellie and Ollie.
They changed color.
And their eyes became enlarged.

"I feel a strong urge to swim far away,"
Ollie said.
"I do, too," Ellie replied.

Something inside the eels was telling them
that a special time had come.

It was time for them to swim to the Sargasso Sea,
many miles away in the ocean.

Ellie and Ollie began that long swim
with many other grown-up eels.

They swam and swam until they came
to the Sargasso Sea.

The eels dived deep down in the water.
Both Ellie and Ollie were very tired.
"I'm worn out," Ellie said.
"But I must release my eggs."

She then released millions
of eggs into the water!
Ollie fertilized them so that they would hatch.
Ellie's and Ollie's important work was done.
Their life cycle was over.

Very tiny eels soon hatched from the eggs.
They didn't look anything like Ellie and Ollie.
They looked like little leaves
and were clear as glass.

The baby eels began a yearlong voyage to America.
They knew that they should go there —
just as Ellie and Ollie had done when they were little.

The baby eels drifted with the Gulf Stream.
As they came near the coast of America,
they changed and began to look like eels.

The young eels, or elvers, returned to the bays and rivers
where their parents had lived.

It was truly a

For they found their new homes
all by themselves!

How did they know that?

The answer is as slippery as an eel!
For no HUMAN really knows for sure.